Wibbly Wobbly Tooth

written by Jay Dale

illustrated by Anna Hancock

Luca had a wibbly wobbly tooth.
It went this way and that.
It went in and out.
Luca could push it all around
but he couldn't pull it out.

"Let me take a look," said Dad happily.
"I'll pull your tooth out for you."

"No thanks, Dad," said Luca.
"I'll pull my tooth out when it's ready.
And I'll pull it out by **myself**!"

"You can't pull it out by yourself,"
said Dad.
"You need my help."

"No!" said Luca.
"I'll do it by myself when it's ready."

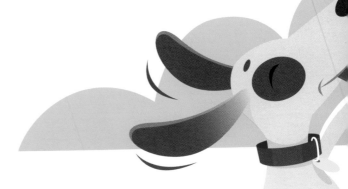

So Luca went on pushing
his wibbly wobbly tooth.
He pushed it this way and that,
and in and out.

The wibbly wobbly tooth felt very wibbly
and very wobbly.
But it didn't hurt at all!

"Come on, Luca," said Grandma.
"What are you waiting for?
You must pull out your tooth today.
It looks ready to come out to me."

"No!" said Luca.
"My tooth is not ready to come out
just yet."

"I'll help you to pull it out," said
Grandma.
"I pulled out your father's tooth
when he was a little boy.
He couldn't pull it out by himself."

"No, thanks," said Luca.
"I'll pull my tooth out when it's ready.
And I'll pull it out by myself!"

So Luca went on pushing and pulling
his tooth.
But his wibbly wobbly tooth
was not ready to come out just yet.
Everyone wanted to help Luca
pull out his tooth.
His mum wanted to help.
His teacher wanted to help.
And his best friend wanted to help, too.

"No!" said Luca to everyone.
"I'll pull out my tooth when it's ready.
And I'll pull it out by myself!"

So Luca tried again.

He pushed his tooth in and out.

It was very, very wobbly.

The tooth went this way and that.

It went in and out.

Luca pushed and pulled it all around.

"Oh!" cried Luca.
"My tooth came out!"
And there in his hand
was his wibbly wobbly tooth.

Luca smiled a great big smile.
"I pulled out my wibbly wobbly tooth!"
he shouted happily to everyone.

"And," he said,
"I pulled it out all by myself —
when it was ready!"